# SUPER BOWL

## ALL-TIME GREATS

BY ANTHONY STREETER

Book design by Jake Slavik
Cover design by Jake Slavik

Photographs ©: Kevin Sabitus/AP Images, cover (top), 1 (top); Greg Trott/AP Images, cover (bottom), 1 (bottom); Bettmann/Getty Images, 4; Focus On Sport/Getty Images Sport/Getty Images, 6, 10, 12, 16; George Gojkovich/Getty Images Sport/Getty Images, 8; E. Bakke/Getty Images Sport/Getty Images, 15; Andy Lyons/Getty Images Sport/Getty Images, 19; Kevin Sabitus/Getty Images Sport/Getty Images, 20

Press Box Books, an imprint of Press Room Editions.

**ISBN**
978-1-63494-865-4 (library bound)
978-1-63494-883-8 (paperback)
978-1-63494-918-7 (epub)
978-1-63494-901-9 (hosted ebook)

**Library of Congress Control Number: 2023923057**

Distributed by North Star Editions, Inc.
2297 Waters Drive
Mendota Heights, MN 55120
www.northstareditions.com

Printed in the United States of America
082024

## ABOUT THE AUTHOR

Anthony Streeter is a former sportswriter who has written for various newspapers. He lives in Columbia, Missouri, with his wife and three kids.

# TABLE OF CONTENTS

STARR
15

## CHAPTER 1
# EARLY DYNASTIES

The National Football League (NFL) began play in 1920. Other leagues tried to challenge the NFL. In the 1960s, one of those leagues became popular. It eventually agreed to join the NFL. The two leagues' champions met after the 1966 season. That game became known as Super Bowl I.

The Green Bay Packers had won the 1965 NFL title. **Bart Starr** kept the winning ways going. The quarterback was smart and consistent. Behind him, the Packers won the first two Super Bowls. Starr was named the game's Most Valuable Player (MVP) each time.

Both wins were easy for the Packers. That was no surprise to NFL fans. They believed the older NFL teams were much better than the new teams. New York Jets quarterback **Joe Namath** disagreed. After the 1968 season, his Jets were big underdogs going into the

Super Bowl. But Namath guaranteed a win. Then he delivered one. It was a stunning loss for the powerful Baltimore Colts.

Three dynasties ruled the 1970s. The Dallas Cowboys reached five Super Bowls. Behind quarterback **Roger Staubach**, they won twice. In the 1971 season, the Miami Dolphins never got going against the Cowboys. Dallas's strong defense and run game dominated. However, Staubach earned MVP honors.

Nobody beat the Dolphins the next year. The 1972 Dolphins became the first undefeated

STAT SPOTLIGHT

## SUPER BOWL RECORD

FEWEST POINTS ALLOWED

**Dallas Cowboys: 3** (January 16, 1972)
**New England Patriots: 3** (February 3, 2019)

Super Bowl champions. Miami's "No-Name Defense" lacked stars. But it shut down opponents. Meanwhile, running back **Larry Csonka** ran for 112 yards in the win. Miami won again the next year. This time Csonka ran for 145 yards and two touchdowns.

No team in the 1970s matched the Pittsburgh Steelers. Pittsburgh won four Super

Bowls from the 1974 to the 1979 seasons. Quarterback **Terry Bradshaw** started all four games. He earned MVP honors twice. Pittsburgh wasn't all about offense, though. Defensive tackle **"Mean" Joe Greene** dominated at the line. And **Jack Lambert** was one of the league's best linebackers. His late interception sealed Pittsburgh's fourth Super Bowl win. Meanwhile, cornerback **Mel Blount** shut down opposing receivers. This trio anchored the Pittsburgh defense for years.

## VINCE LOMBARDI

Since the 1970 season, Super Bowl champions have received the Vince Lombardi Trophy. The trophy is named after the legendary coach of the Green Bay Packers. Green Bay had been a losing team in the 1950s. Then Lombardi arrived. He led the Packers to three NFL titles from 1961 to 1965. Then they won the first two Super Bowls.

UPSHAW
63

CHAPTER 2

# LEGENDS

The Raiders reached four of the first 18 Super Bowls. They won three of them. The team's powerful offensive line played a big role. Few defenders ever got past guard **Gene Upshaw** and tackle **Art Shell**. They helped the Raiders win two championships while the team was in Oakland.

Things weren't as successful across the bay. The San Francisco 49ers had never won a championship. Then quarterback **Joe Montana** arrived. From 1981 to 1989, the 49ers won four Super Bowls. Montana's steady play was a major reason why. Known

as "Joe Cool," Montana won the MVP Award in three of the wins. The last came in the 1989 season. The opposing Denver Broncos boasted a tough defense. But they were no match for Montana. He passed for 297 yards and five touchdowns. The 49ers won 55–10.

Montana threw many of his passes to Jerry Rice. The star receiver was there for two of San Francisco's championship seasons in the 1980s. Then, after Montana left, he helped the 49ers win another title in the 1994 season. Rice's skills were unmatched. When he retired, he held almost every major Super Bowl receiving record.

The Dallas Cowboys returned to glory in the early 1990s. After the 1992 season, Troy Aikman dominated in the Super Bowl. The quarterback earned MVP honors by throwing four touchdown passes. Wide receiver Michael Irvin caught two of

## JOE GIBBS

Joe Gibbs took over as Washington's coach in 1981. Over the next 12 years, he led the team to three Super Bowl wins. A different quarterback started each game. No other coach has done that.

those touchdowns. The next season, **Emmitt Smith** won the Super Bowl MVP Award. The running back ran for 132 yards and two touchdowns. The "Triplets" of Aikman, Irvin, and Smith led the Cowboys to three Super Bowl wins in four years.

**Charles Haley** played for both dynasties. He won two Super Bowls as a bruising linebacker with the 49ers. Then he moved to defensive end for all three Cowboys wins. He became the first player to win five Super Bowls.

The Broncos lost three Super Bowls in the 1980s. **John Elway** played quarterback in

STAT SPOTLIGHT

**SUPER BOWL RECORD**

RECEIVING YARDS IN A GAME

**Jerry Rice: 215** (January 22, 1989)

all three. In 1997, Elway led the Broncos back to the big game. Running back **Terrell Davis** broke out that year as well. An injury kept Davis out the entire second quarter of the Super Bowl. But he still rushed for a record three touchdowns in an upset win. The next year was Elway's last. He went out on a high note. The veteran had one passing touchdown and one rushing touchdown in a comfortable 34–19 win over the Atlanta Falcons.

WARNER
13

# CHAPTER 3
# MODERN STARS

At first, no NFL team wanted quarterback **Kurt Warner**. He worked in a grocery store to make ends meet. Finally, in 1998, the St. Louis Rams signed him as a backup. Warner eventually became the spark for an all-time great offense in 1999. That season's Super Bowl came down to the final play. St. Louis held on to win. Warner's 414 passing yards set a Super Bowl record. He also threw two touchdown passes in an MVP performance.

Few teams put up big numbers against the 2000 Baltimore Ravens. In that season's Super Bowl, the New York Giants scored only seven points against them. And the Ravens forced five turnovers in the win. **Ray Lewis** led a powerful Baltimore defense. The aggressive middle linebacker dominated all over the field and earned the MVP Award. It was the first of two championships for Lewis and the Ravens.

Quarterback **Tom Brady** began the 2001 season as a backup. By the end of the 2004 season, he had led his team to three Super Bowl wins. Brady eventually won a record sixth Super Bowl. All came with the New England Patriots. Then he added one more with the Tampa Bay Buccaneers.

STAT SPOTLIGHT

**SUPER BOWL RECORD**

CAREER PASSING YARDS

**Tom Brady: 3,039**

Big moments never seemed to faze Brady. After the 2016 season, his team trailed 28–3 in the Super Bowl. Brady led the Patriots all the way back. They won 34–28 in overtime. Brady's name is all over the Super Bowl record books. And no player has won as many as his five Super Bowl MVPs. **Rob Gronkowski** was Brady's favorite target. The athletic tight end played in five Super Bowls with Brady, winning three.

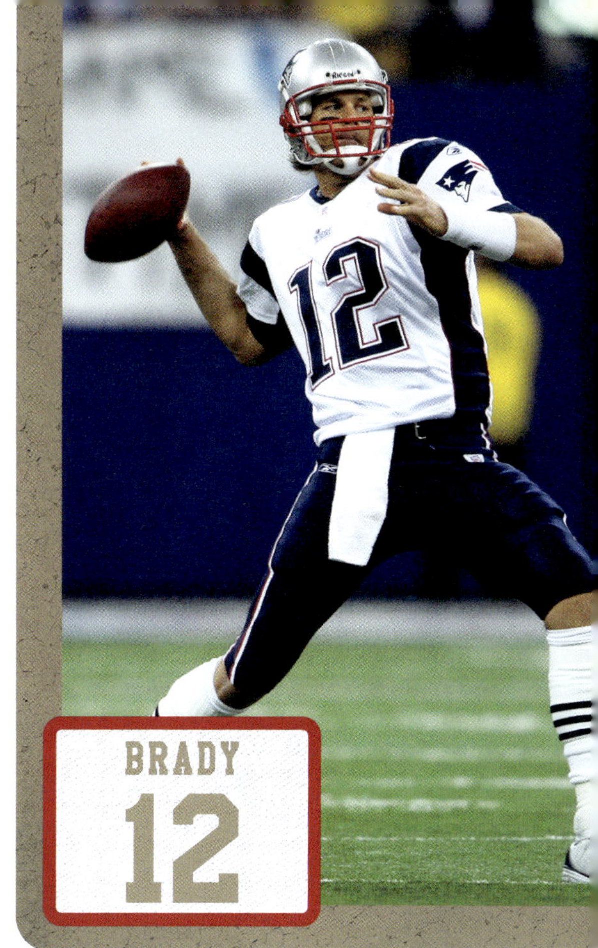


Kicker **Adam Vinatieri** shined in four Super Bowl wins. Three came with

New England. Twice, he kicked game-winning field goals for the Patriots.

The Seattle Seahawks reached the Super Bowl in the 2013 season. The team's defense boasted hard-hitting safety **Kam Chancellor**. He recorded 10 tackles and an interception in Seattle's 43–8 win over Denver. Seahawks linebacker **Bobby Wagner** had 12 tackles and an interception in the next season's Super Bowl. However, Seattle fell one play short of a second championship.

**Patrick Mahomes** grew up playing baseball. His powerful arm helped create a new dynasty in Kansas City. The elite quarterback led the Chiefs to four Super Bowls in five years. They won after the 2019, 2022, and 2023 seasons. Mahomes was named MVP each time.

## THE MANNING BROTHERS

Peyton Manning led the Indianapolis Colts and Denver Broncos to Super Bowl wins. Most football fans consider him one of the best quarterbacks ever. However, Peyton's younger brother, Eli Manning, holds Super Bowl bragging rights. Eli also won two Super Bowls. Both came with the New York Giants. But Eli claimed two Super Bowl MVPs. Peyton earned only one.

# TIMELINE

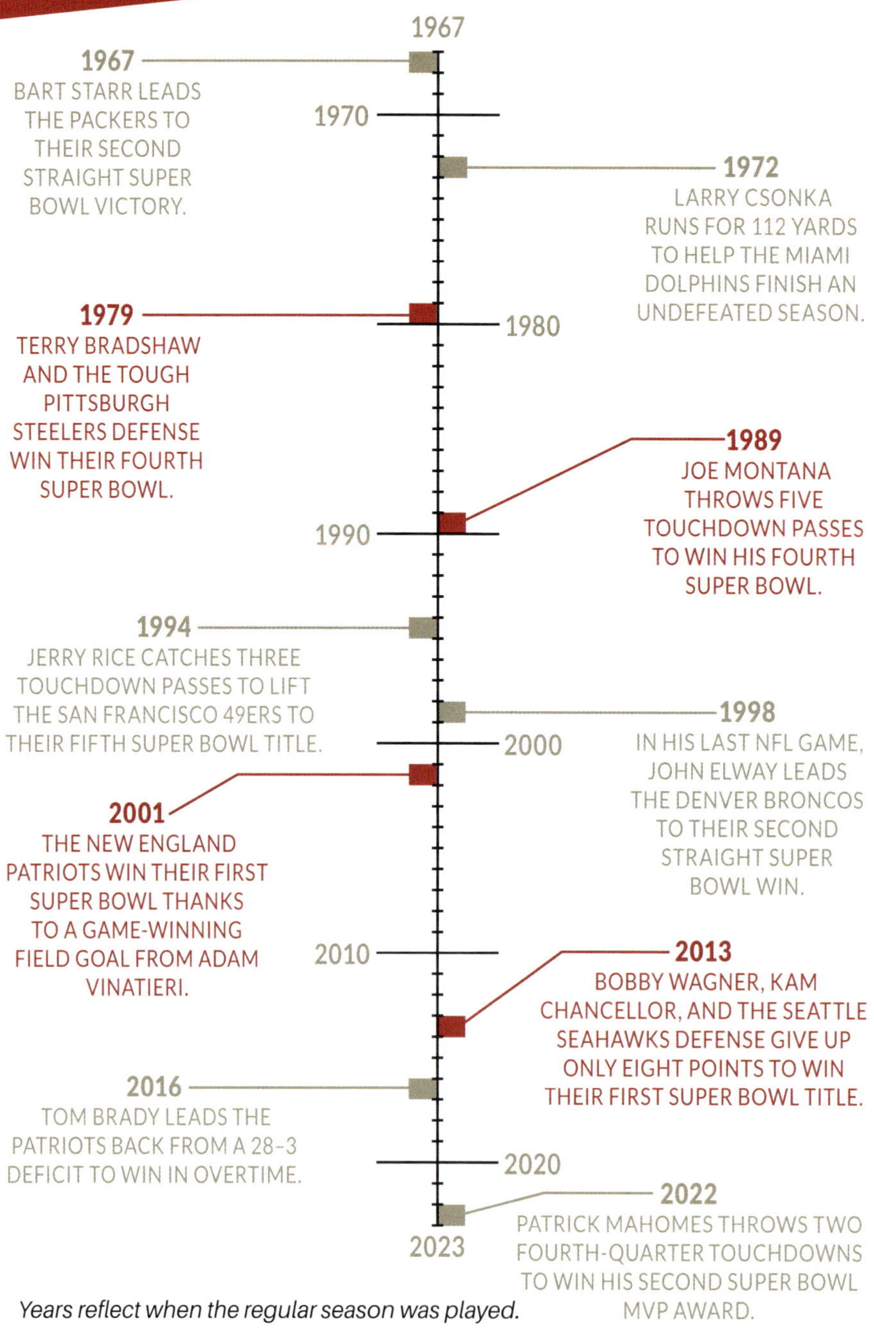


*Years reflect when the regular season was played.*

# CHAMPIONSHIP FACTS

## SUPER BOWL

**First played:** January 15, 1967

**Most titles as a player:** Tom Brady, 7

**Most titles as a coach:** Bill Belichick, 6

**Most titles by a team:** New England Patriots and Pittsburgh Steelers, 6

*Stats are accurate through the 2023 season.*

### MORE INFORMATION

To learn more about the Super Bowl, go to **pressboxbooks.com/AllAccess**.

These links are routinely monitored and updated to provide the most current information available.

# GLOSSARY

**aggressive**
Making an all-out effort to win.

**dynasties**
Teams that have extended periods of success, usually winning multiple championships in the process.

**elite**
The best of the best.

**guaranteed**
Promised.

**interception**
A play in which the defense catches a pass and gains possession of the ball.

**offensive line**
The players who block for running backs and stop defenders from reaching the quarterback.

**undefeated**
Not having any losses.

**underdogs**
Individuals or teams that are not expected to win.

**upset**
When a weaker team or player unexpectedly wins.

**veteran**
A player who has spent several years in a league.

# INDEX